SHADOW OF THUNDER

SHADOW OF THUNDER
by Max Evans

THE SWALLOW PRESS INC.
CHICAGO

Illustrations by Victor Seper/Chicago
Photographic assistance by Vincent Lucarelli

Published by The Swallow Press Incorporated
1139 South Wabash Avenue   Chicago, Illinois 60605

Library of Congress Catalog Card Number 69-20469

For Jack and Dorothy
Brandenburg of the First
State Bank of Taos, and Charles
Crowder of Albuquerque.
They all know why.

She saw the wagon coming along the road followed by a man on horseback. Two matching bays pulled it and the man who trailed behind was mounted on a pinto. As the vehicle rolled nearer she could see the figure on the wagon seat was dressed in dark purple from his wide felt hat to the long-tailed coat on down to his high-topped boots. The mounted man was an Indian. Apache.

She smoothed her hands down her dress front and over her high pitched breasts, then straightened her long hair—hair as shiny blue-black as the mane of the pinto.

The man pulled back on the reins, saying quietly, "Whoa." He dismounted and tied the reins to the wagon wheel. Then he strode towards the porch. He was not as big as he had seemed sitting up on the wagon. Actually he was of medium height but his arms hung long and the hands at their ends were outsized. His walk was one of certainty and purpose as if every step he took must count.

Marta Ames stared curiously out her very dark, shining eyes. An unknown feeling stroked across her body ever so lightly. A few goose bumps pimpled on the white, fair skin of her rounded forearms. Her lavender red lips parted slightly. Visitors were few out here, and mostly they came to talk cows with her husband.

This one was different. She stepped back from the front door as he raised a heavy hand to knock. She waited a moment then opened it. The eyes she looked into were darker than her own and the skin was almost as white. It was evident that this man didn't spend too much time under the sunburned sky. His lips were thin but moist. His face was also thin and his firm set jaw showed small, permanent muscle knots.

"How do you do, fair lady? I fear I've lost my way. I look

for the road to the city of Two Mesas."

She started to answer and give directions, but he went on in a voice deep but smooth, like the flowing of pure water over fine silk.

"Perchance the gods have cast favorable glances at my humble wagon, for where else would one meet such lovely and charming female flesh? Where else indeed?"

The blood pushed the redness under Marta's white skin. "Well, I . . . . ," she started, but again the honeyed words flowed out.

"Do not be taken aback by my words. I do not mean to be forward but I was greatly surprised to meet one of such extreme beauty here in the wilderness. Is the man of the house about?"

"Why yes, he and Marcus are doctoring cattle out in the corral," she said.

"Sickness?" he asked.

"Only a few head," she answered.

"My card," he said reaching long fingers into his inner coat while with the other hand sweeping his hat from his thick-haired head.

Marta took it and read: DUVALL—DOCTOR OF THE MIND AND BODY. GIFTED WITH A MULTITUDE OF DIVINE ABILITIES.

"I am Duvall," he said, holding a hand out to her.

For a moment she hesitated, then boldly took it. The soft hugeness of it enveloped hers in a warm, almost but not quite, damp embrace. The bumps came again. This time she felt them over all her body.

"If I might be so bold could I ask for a cup of water? The road has been long and my thirst is great."

"Surely. Come in," she said, flashing a look at the Indian now dismounted and squatting by the wagon.

In answer to her look he said, "Never mind him, he's like a camel of the desert. One Lion is an Apache. He's trained in the ways of the desert."

She handed him the tin dipper from the wooden bucket. He took the cool water to himself in long, smooth swallows.

"Now," he said, wiping the drippings from the corner of his mouth with a blue silk handkerchief, "I shall repay this golden kindness by assisting your husband in the corrals."

Rick Ames spurred the appaloosa gelding after the white-faced yearling. When the distance was just right he whirled the catch-rope and let the loop fly. It sailed out and around the yearling's head. Rick jerked the slack out of the loop and turned, spurring the gelding in the opposite direction. The rope tightened and spun the yearling around, his four feet planted stiff, and bawling at the top of his voice.

Marcus, the Mexican cowhand, reined in and dropped a slow loop under the calf's belly and up against its hind legs. The legs moved into the loop. He, too, jerked the slack and rode in the opposite direction from Rick. The calf was flopped hard upon the ground, stretched out flat.

Quickly the appaloosa turned his head down the rope, holding it tight, as Rick dismounted. He moved to the side of the corral and picked up a flat smooth stock, a small bottle of chloroform, and a can of pine tar. With practiced motion he poured the chloroform into the cavity where the calf had recently been dehorned. At the touch of the liquid the worms wiggled and twisted up out of the rotting wound. He scooped them all out with the wooden spatula, then coated the sore with the pine tar.

They turned the yearling loose. It got up shaking its head in the corral dust and ambled off addled but in much better health.

Rick liked things on his ranch to be in shape. He kept his fences tight and well cared for, his cows doctored and fat. His horses were the best in the country. Appaloosas. Indians long before bred these spotted-rumped animals for their toughness and endurance over the long haul.

He pushed his hat back over his forehead which was paste white in comparison to the bronze skin on the rest of his face. A shock of light brown hair showed beneath the brim.

"It's going to get hot early this year, huh, Marcus?"

"Looks like," answered Marcus in a heavy Mexican accent. "Maybe so we got the cows moved to the forest lease just in time, no?"

"Yeah, looks like they'll get an early start. Should be licking themselves and piling on the fat right now."

He straightened his six-foot-one frame and stared out of light brown, steady eyes at the yearling steer standing in the corner with the wide swelled belly and the watery red eyes. Marcus stood leaning against the corral pulling smoke deep into his lungs. His eyes followed those of his boss.

"What we do about that water-belly steer?" he asked.

"I don't know, Marcus. I've never saved one yet. Looks like this one's goin' to be a goner in another couple of days. Cain't figure it out. It only happens once ever two or three years. Last time we lost six head. Something about the water makes a rock form in their bladder. Then they pass it down into their pecker and that's that. The water all backs up and pretty soon there's no room for grass or fresh water either. Then it's just a matter of a few days until they're done."

"What cause this . . . this pecker stopping?" asked Marcus, frowning in the bright sun. "You think maybe he got a dose of clap? Huh?"

"I don't know," Rick grinned. "Old man Randall said it was calcium in the water that caused it to form. I just cain't understand it. Oh well, no matter what, a feller can always count on a ten percent stock loss. Hell, you could raise 'em in the kitchen and you'd lose the same percentage."

He saw the wagon pull up in front and wondered where old Ring the dog was. He usually barked when company came. *Guess he's off hunting*, he thought to himself. The wagon pulled out of sight, hidden by the house. Well, whoever it was Marta'd send them on out to the corral.

Marta. At the thought of her he had that funny, mellow feeling. He'd never get over it. He knew that, now. They'd been married seven years and he still got it every time he thought of her. There was just one thing he was more proud of than his spotted-rumped horses and that was Marta.

By damn, he was lucky — a good little ranch, several hundred head of well-bred cattle to go on it; it was fenced and cross-fenced so he could rotate his cattle and not eat any one pasture down too close to the ground — and the most beautiful woman in the world to fix his meals, take care of the chickens, the garden, sew, and take him to bed. All paid for, too. In fact, that's how he'd gotten Marta.

It was a regular business deal, like trading for a bunch of good springing heifers. He'd showed what he owned, what he made every year, and pointed out to her, and her family, all the advantages of marrying up with Rick Ames. She'd taken

him up on it. As if she could refuse a deal like that.

There was just one thing missing though. No kids. He wanted that very much. He reckoned it was Marta's fault. She must have been born barren. Well, too bad. One of these days if she didn't do her duty in that line why they'd just adopt one. Some nester gal over on Salt River was always getting in a family way and would be mighty glad to have a place to put a young 'un like that. He'd give her one more year though. Maybe she'd come through.

"I hear Tony Archuleta lost four two-year-olds last week." Rick said to Marcus.

"Whooooeee," Marcus said, "Four head. Sone of a beetch. Tony ees always loosin' them young heifers. What cause it, Reeck? Huh? What cause it? Tony hees take very good care of his stock. I know this for chure. Huh?"

"I've told him and told him not to feed too much grain to springing heifers. They get too fat around the hips and they can't force the calf out. Why, old Tony spends three-fourths of his time pullin' calves in the spring. I bet he loses fifty percent of his two-year-old calves every year. There ain't no use in tryin' to explain to him, Marcus. He thinks that the fatter anything is, the healthier."

"Whoooeeee, I say he chure does. Look at Rosita. She's always fat and always having the bambinos. No?"

"Yeah, women are different. Looks like the fatter they get the easier it is to shell out."

"Say, Reeck, when you goin' to start making the young ones? Huh?"

Rick swallowed and looked away as he said, "It's about time ain't it? At least I got me a woman to start on. That's more'n you can say."

"You right, Reeck, I'm goin' to get me a big, skinny bones so she won't be sloughing no bambinos. Huh? I tell you, Reeck, I tell you something fonny. I already got me two leetle ones." Marcus looked around, then whispered so quietly that the saints probably had to strain to hear. "You know Maria Sanchez at Two Mesas?"

"Yeah."

"Thass her. Thass the one. Both little bulls handsome like the papa, no?"

Rick saw them coming. The figures in a triangle. Marta and the dark clad stranger walking abreast and the huge Apache following behind. It was strange, he thought, Marta never came to the corrals unless he asked her to. As they neared he noticed how much smaller the man was than he'd first thought.

Marta said, "Rick, this is Mr. Duvall. Mr. Duvall, my husband, Rick Ames."

He took the huge hand and even his rope- and saddle-stretched hand was swallowed.

"Your wife has been so kind to proffer my parched and dust-raw throat a cup of the most gratifying liquid. In return I thought I might contribute some of my small, but heaven-sent, gift of healing to your sick cattle."

"Thanks," said Rick, feeling somehow resentful. "I reckon we've done about all that can be done."

"What about the one standing there so evidently afflicted with what the layman calls the waterbelly?"

"Aw, that one's already gone. Besides even the vet cain't do nothin' about that."

"My dear Mr. Ames, I am not a veterinarian," and with a great sweep of his arm he offered his card to Rick.

"Well . . . . what do you think you could do for *that* yearlin'?" He said it as a question, but he meant it as a challenge.

Duvall turned to the Apache and spoke in Indian. The Apache stared ahead. He didn't seem to focus his eyes on anything in particular. It was almost as if he were dead except for some lonely living cell that moved only when Duvall spoke.

The Indian was dressed in the way of the Apache, almost knee-high moccasins with a drawstring around the ankles. The long square-bottomed shirt hung down over britches split up each leg and partially laced with buckskin string. He wore a wide belt around his middle and a red rag tied around his head to keep the heavy, shoulder-length hair pulled out of his face. Expressionless, the Apache turned and walked swiftly back to the wagon.

"The Apaches," Duvall said, in answer to the look on Rick's face, "are fine people. I have a large debt to them in much of my knowledge of healing. Now," he said, pulling off the long dark coat and folding it neatly atop the corral, "I presume you have chloroform, seeing as you have been doctoring for worms."

"Yeah," said Rick walking over and picking up the bottle.

"Now, if you don't mind, I'd like you to throw the steer and hold him in any manner you deem suitable."

"What're you goin' to do?" asked Rick, humping up just a little.

"You want to save this poor creature, do you now?"

"Well . . . . ."

"You have nothing to lose, is that not correct?"

"Yeah, I reckon . . . . ."

"Then let's begin."

Marcus joined Rick and they threw the steer into the ground-up dust and manure of the corral. Rick pulled a foreleg up with his knee on the steer's shoulder. Marcus took the tail and stretched it back between the widespread hind legs. The sick animal put up very little struggle. Its swollen belly stuck up high and the pressure of its weight made the breath come hard. Little furrows were plowed in the corral dust by the breathing and some of it collected around the wet nostrils.

Smoothly Duvall took a pure white handkerchief from inside a black silk one and poured a small amount of chloroform on it. Then he held it over the steer's nostrils, counting as he did so.

The Apache returned and without a word handed Duvall the square-bottomed, leather bag. Duvall nodded at a place by his side and continued counting. Then he finished. He opened the bag. Taking out a long handled, steel knife with a very short and very sharp blade. He poured something out of a bottle on the protruding penis of the steer, rubbing it all over the stomach and up between its legs.

"What's that?" asked Rick.

"Its main ingredient is the oil of sagebrush," answered Duvall. "It has other things in it. Sage oil is a wonderful healing agent and disinfectant."

"I knew the Indians drank it for colds," said Rick, "but I didn't know it was good for anything else."

"Few do, Mr. Ames. Most of us are blind to all the wonderful healing agents nature has laid at our very doorsteps." He set three other bottles out of the bag, and he arranged them in proper order. Then he took a needle and heavy thread and laid them out on a piece of soft leather.

The steer breathed now without struggling. Duvall picked a spot behind the penis and deftly split through the skin and flesh all the way to the inner penis in three swift strokes. The blood poured out on the hide and trickled down through the red and white hairs to the dirt. He opened a wide cut, mopping the blood up now and then with an absorbent cloth. He cut the penis. His hands, covered with red now, worked magically, large and flexible with certain knowledge of what his mind told them to do.

Marta stood still, pale. Her eyes were fixed to the gaping insides of the steer.

Duvall cut the penis out, took the bladder and sewed it to another smaller split farther back between the steer's legs. The stitching took longer than all the rest. He tied a knot in the end of the string. Cut it. Then he poured a portion of bitter smelling greenish colored liquid into the wound and sewed the first cut up. He then inserted a small piece of hollow bone in the second hole.

"That's it," he said.

Rick felt the sweat rolling from under his hat and he wiped at the saltiness of it where it was getting in his eyes.

Marcus got up stiffly and backed to the corral, leaning weakly, staring hard at Duvall.

Duvall said calmly as he split the long, narrow, red penis apart, "We should find the culprit here." With the end of the blood-gummed knife he picked the hard pebble-like formation out and held it for all to see. Then he spoke, "The swelling will hold that piece of bone in place for a few days. When the swelling is gone enough for the bone to drop out, the animal will be healed sufficiently to do without it. You no longer have a steer, Mr. Ames. You now, for all practical purposes, except breeding, have a heifer. But a live heifer is much more to your advantage than a dead steer."

Rick Ames had watched the unheard-of skill of Duvall's

hands perform a miraculous operation. He was stunned. He spoke, "I don't know what to say."

"Never mind," said Duvall raising a wide-spread, red-stained hand. "Never mind. It is enough reward to have the ability."

Marta looked at the mighty hand. Her nostrils flared a little more than before and a deep gleaming light seemed to crowd its way to the misty surface of her eyes. Her breathing raised her breasts in and out, up and down.

"Now if you will be so kind to show me to a wash basin we will be soon on our way."

He washed his hands several times, then applied a grey, cool-looking lotion, almost tenderly. He spoke once more as he donned his coat, "My friends, if you would honor me a week from today with your presence at our little musical to be held somewhere in the vicinity of Two Mesas, I will leave with happiness in my heart and a glow of appreciation over all my being."

"We're the ones to appreciate," said Rick.

"We'll come," said Marta softly.

"Then I leave you with this in mind, good people. If perchance you should need help with your mind or body please call upon Duvall." He strode out to his wagon, untied the reins, mounted easily and drove the wagon away. The Apache followed close behind.

Marta stood as yet in one spot and Rick looked out the back porch and saw that indeed the old dog had been there all the time. He stood motionless, soundless, and sniffed the air.

Rick stretched and stapled a fence line tight and returned the tools to a saddle pouch.

He untracked Brother Bill, his appaloosa, mounted and rode down off the hill towards the water gap in the sandy draw. He was sure the heavy rains day before yesterday had washed it out. Brother Bill walked along fox-trotting and chewing at the bits. He was full of life and wanted to work.

"Okay, Brother Bill, in about three weeks, me and Marcus will take some of this spunk outa you when we go up on the forest land to brand."

Marcus was up there now taking a count of the mother cows and calves, locating their watering places so they could be gathered in a hurry when they were ready for the branding. They still had about thirty or forty more head to brand, counting the late calves yet to be born.

The day was clear and the sunlight sparkled in the air from the lush dampness all about. The grass was deep green and growing with a swift tenderness.

The water gap *had* pulled loose on one side and the three wires were strung along the draw with dirt, sticks, and dead grass all entangled in it. He pulled the wires free, dragged them across the draw, and tied them back after resetting the heavy cedar post. Then he retied the rock weights out in the middle so it would pull the wires down to the ground. His pastures were back in shape again.

With a feeling of satisfaction, he mounted up and rode towards the low-lying ranch house, thinking of Marta and the good meal she would have ready.

Then he saw a horse-backer riding down the road that led into the ranch proper. He could tell, even from that distance, by the way he sat his horse, that it was his neighbor to the north, old man George Randall. George was stiff as a cedar post and just as tough. He had merry, watery-blue eyes, that had gazed into a lot of hot and cold winds; many dry years had wrinkled his skin like the bark of a pine tree. He always timed his rides in this direction to catch a meal of Marta's, claiming her to be the best cook around.

They came together riding in a V at the ranch gate.

"Howdy, George," Rick said, smiling, glad to see his weathered old friend.

"Whatcha say, Rick? Looks like I timed it just right. Marta oughta have the chuck on the table 'bout now."

"You sure did, George. Tie your horse and come on in."

George tied the roan he was riding, while Rick turned his horse loose in the corral. Together they walked to the back porch and into the kitchen. The smell of fresh fried beef was evident and Marta was just taking the biscuits out of the oven.

"Hello, George. How's Frieda?"

"Aw, she's just like any other old woman, always bellyachin' and makin' it miserable for me," he laughed good-naturedly.

"I bet you wouldn't take for her though," said Marta.

"Well, I reckon she does come in handy around the place."

"That's how all you ranchers feel about your women," said Marta, only half teasing.

"Sit down, George, and help yourself to the chow," Rick said. "How're your cows doin'?"

"Sure comin' along good this year. I believe my calves will pass four hundred pounds apiece come shipping time. Sure hope the price holds up till fall. Dang, I wish we could get the rail-spur on into Two Mesas. It takes lots of beef off makin' that drive to Stanton."

"Well, old man Ords got a petition signed by every cowman in the country. If the goddamned nesters would sign we could probably get it through," said Rick.

"Yeah, but they won't. They ain't got over the war yet."

The war referred to by Randall had been over for several years now, but neither side forgot. The nesters had moved in all over the West, homesteading farms along river bottoms and around water holes, settling one-hundred-and-sixty acre plots. The nesters were within the law, but the ranchers felt that morally they themselves were in the right. The ranchers resented the land being broken up into little pieces; it undercut their entire system of ranching. Range wars and killings spread across the land. Finally, nature took care of the nesters who had fought the dry-land farms. They were simply starved out and the ranchers took over the land again. But along Salt River it was different. Here they got a little irrigation water and farmed small patches of vegetables and kept milk cows, chickens, and hogs. They made an existence; that was all they could boast. Such was also the relationship now between the ranchers and the nesters; it was an existence, an impasse; few could boast of friendship.

"They don't ship enough cattle to count—or care," Rick said bitterly. "All they keep is a bunch of hogs and a milk cow around them sodbustin' flats over on Salt River. Too damn bad. Oh well," he added, "I look for all them nesters to starve out anyway in another five years."

"I hope so," said Randall.

Marta pushed the curl from her forehead and finished setting the meal of pinto beans, fried beef, home-canned peaches, hot biscuits, and country butter. They set to and drank deep swallows of hot coffee from the large tin cups.

Marta wished Rick could see his way clear to let her order some china cups. But he kept putting all his money in cows. 'Spreading out,' as he said. 'A man's got to spread out while he's goin' good.'

The talk went on, cows, cows, cows, horses, and more cows. She liked cows. She liked ranch life, but an unknown craving for some spice to go with it gnawed at her breast. Maybe that get-together of Duvall's would give them something else to think about for a change. Duvall, what a strange and fascinating man. Where did he come from? What was he really? Marta wondered.

"Marta, when you and old Rick goin' to get some younguns around here?"

Rick felt the red creep into his face. *My god, why did everybody have to bring that up lately?*

George went on jokingly, "If I wasn't so cockeyed old I'd do you a good neighborly turn and help you out, Rick." George bellowed across a fork full of beef.

Rick grinned, "I'll let you know if I need any help," he said lamely.

After the filling meal, they rolled smokes and talked on as Marta cleared the table and prepared to wash the dishes. A big pan of water was heating on the iron range, its steam wiggling up into the kitchen.

George spent a couple of hours rolling smokes and talking more cows, then he got up, thanked Marta for the fine feed, and rode on west where he too had a lease from the forest for grazing purposes.

Rick sat and finished his last smoke. "Well, I reckon I'll go out and patch the corrals. I noticed a few loose posts the other day when that Duvall feller was working on the yearlin'."

Marta put down the dish she was drying. She said, "Have you forgotten what day it is?"

Rick thought hard — *anniversary? birthday?* "I . . . I . . . don't know, honey. What day is it?"

"You mean you don't know after what he did for us?"

"Oh, you mean Duvall? That's right, this is the night for the big meeting. I'd plumb forgot."

"We'll have to get started soon because I have some things to get in town," she said.

"All right, I'll go out and warm up the truck. I don't need to shave seeing as how I just did this morning."

In a little while Rick returned to the house. He was stunned at the sight of his wife. He had never seen her done up so pretty. The heavy black hair was all tied high in a bundle on top of her head. She wore a lavender dress and a black half-coat. And a big silver comb was stuck in her hair. Her lips were coated with lavender paint to match the dress. Her eyes glowed bright and excited out at him as she waited for his comment.

"You're as pretty as a peach tree in new bloom, Marta." She smiled slightly. "You like the dress?" She asked.

"Like it? It's the prettiest thing I ever saw in my life — except maybe the woman in it." He smiled. "That Duvall ought to be mighty proud to have the likes of you attending his meetin'. Say, by the way, I saw that yearlin' this morning. Most of the swelling's gone and he's eatin' good. You know, Marta, I just cain't figure it out. I've never heard of anything like what he did to that steer. It just ain't natural. There's something plumb spooky about the way he operated on that animal."

"There's probably lots of things we haven't heard about in this world, Rick."

They bounded along in the creaking truck; every now and then Marta straightened her hair from the jostling it took as they struck innumerable holes and ruts in the dirt road.

"Rick, don't you think it's about time we bought a car? This old truck is for hauling fence posts and baled hay."

"It's a lot faster than a buggy."

"The day of the buggy is over."

"If a buggy was good enough for my dad and his pa, a truck is fine for us. When they pioneered the first cow ranch in this country there were no roads at all. This road we're travelin' right now was first a cow trail, then a wagon trail, then a buggy trail, and here we are sailin' along over it at twenty miles an hour."

"I really don't call this sailing," said Marta. She was racked against the door by an especially deep hole.

"Nobody's ever satisfied in this world," Rick said.

Marta said, "It's not that we can't afford it. We got through the depression and the drouth better than anybody around."

"Well, that's because I hadn't gone in debt for a bunch of things we didn't need and had all that hay stored in case of an emergency."

"I know," she said, "but it's different now. We have money in the bank. The grass is good this year."

"Yeah, but you never know about next year."

"You can't just go on thinking about next year. We're alive

now. Right now in nineteen hundred and thirty seven, in the beautiful month of June."

"Look, a wagon and team is still good enough for this Duvall."

"That's for effect," she said. "I want a car for comfort and because I get tired and embarrassed driving this truck like a hayhand to social gatherings."

"A woman as good lookin' as you could go to a social on a hundred-year-old mule and they'd all be glad to have her."

"You just don't understand," she said resignedly, "You never will."

They drove into the farming and ranching town of Two Mesas. It was half adobe structures and half crude, box-like, frame houses—some with no paint, others with a little, clinging to the weathered boards. A reminder of someone's attempt at beauty in a land hot and dry in the summer, and so cold and wind-cursed in the winter that paint was only a wasted gesture.

Old cars and trucks stood about. A few wagons and teams were tied here and there. And once in a great while a new car stood out saying for the owner to all, 'the drouth is over, I've made a crop. I believe in the land again.'

Rick pulled up in front of the Allen Hardware to get some ranch supplies. Marta got the few essential grocery purchases made in the mercantile then walked across the street to Berg's Dry Goods.

Berg welcomed her with, "Ah, Mrs. Ames, you look like all the flowers in the world today. Is there a reason for such beauty? No, no," he went on, "just let it be. Let us accept this bounty without question. How is Mr. Ames?"

"Just fine. Working hard as usual."

"Did you come in for the camp meeting or whatever it is?"

"Yes, and to do some shopping."

"Good, good," Mr. Berg said, and he rubbed his little pot belly, took off his glasses and pointed to a hanging of new dresses.

"That yellow one was just made for you. You alone."

Marta fingered the soft, frilly dress as yellow as a new ray of sun beaming through a deep, green forest. She wanted it. For a frivolous moment she craved it, then she said, "I'd like to look at some material." She knew Rick would be irritated for days if she bought the dress when she could easily make one of her own. She did pick out a yellow cloth as near that of the ready-made as possible. She chose a pattern and bought the thread and everything she'd need to make the dress. Suddenly she was determined to design one that would cause the other to look secondhand.

"If you made the dress you're wearing, it is easy to understand why a factory dress, even one as fine as that," he pointed again at the yellow dress, "would seem awkward and ugly to you."

Marta blushed a little at this flattery and said, "Yes, I did. I made it, thank you."

Mr. Berg put all the purchases in a sack. Marta paid by check. She made it out to the exact cent and wrote on it each item purchased. This, too, would please Rick. Even though the actual expense of the material had been almost as much as the new ready-to-wear dress would have cost.

"How's the family, Mr. Berg?"

"Oh, fine, fine, except Mama's got the gout again. Always gets it right after the first summer rains. Makes her hungry. She eats far too much you know. Mama's big, big!" He made a proud measurement with his little arms.

"And the children?"

"Well, they work in the store evenings. We stay open till nine now you know. Abie doesn't like it. He only likes the violin. He has a mail-order course. Miss Bridge, the music teacher at school, says he's 'gifted'."

"I'd like to hear him play sometime. There are very few gifted people around Two Mesas."

"Oh, fine, fine, I'll tell him. He'll be pleased."

Marta told him goodbye as Berg followed her out on the wooden porch thanking her effusively for her trade.

Rick was loading some wire and other ranch goods in the back of the truck.

"Come on," he said, "let's go over to Lil's and have some coffee."

They walked together and she told him about the dress material she'd bought and that she intended to make it up right away so she could wear it to the next camp meeting.

"The next one?" he said. "How do you know you'll like this one?"

"Well, it's something different to do. A change."

He looked at her, starting to speak, but held it back as they entered Lil's Cafe.

Lil was right there. "It's about time you kids came into town near sundown. I ain't seen you in this late for months."

"Goin' to the meetin' or whatever it is," Rick said.

"That's twice today I've heard 'whatever it is'," said Marta.

"What?" said Rick.

"Nothing."

Lil folded her heavy arms under her heavier breasts, and said, smiling from a round pleasant face, "Now don't tell me you're goin' to just have coffee. It's not too long till supper time, and I've got some roast beef that'd make a well-fed prisoner break slap out of jail just to get one teeny little bite."

"Anything that good is worth waitin' for. Coffee first, Lil, and then the roast beef. All right, Honey?" Rick asked.

Marta nodded, amazed that he'd buy a meal. He always worked it so they got into town in the afternoon, shopped fast, and drove home for supper. Maybe there was hope yet.

When Lil served the meal, Marta learned the reason for his new generosity.

"Say, Lil, been any cow buyers in town yet?"

"There's two here now. They'll be gettin' around to you after old man Moss, I reckon."

"What're they buyin'?"

"Calves for fall delivery. Makin' a guaranteed offer on 'em now."

After Lil left, Rick cut at his beef smiling, "You know what that means, honey?"

"What?" she said dryly.

"That means cattle are goin' to go up this fall, in the eyes of the experts at least. I ain't contractin' a single head."

Marta sipped her coffee a moment before eating, and watched Rick devour his beef in great bites. *Just like he wants to devour me*, she suddenly thought. *I'm only good to give him strength to run his damned ranch and make it grow, grow, grow.*

Lil spoke from behind the counter where she served several cowhands, "The meeting's down by Salt River. Guess this Duvall didn't figure any of you ranchers would come, so he's playing up to the nesters and garden farmers."

"They need preachin' to worse than we do anyhow," Rick said.

"It seems that poor folks always need preaching to worse than the well off," Marta said quietly.

"Aw, come on, you're getting on edge for no reason."

Rick got up to join several of the hands who were talking, here and there, about grass and all that goes with ranching. Marta sat alone staring out the window at more and more people coming into Two Mesas for the meeting. Even so, she thought the town was still lonely and dead. She was relieved when Rick came over and said, "It's about time for the great meetin'. Let's go."

The old truck rattled out of town towards Salt River about a mile from the city limits. Rick drove along the winding road where dust hung in the air from the vehicles ahead of them.

"I never saw such a crowd at an opening before," he said. "Later on, yes, but never before the word got out."

People were coming in old, worn-out cars that wheezed and jerked. Some were horseback and others came by wagon and team, blocking the road so the cars had to stop or pull around. Some were ranchers; most were nesters.

The Salt River nesters turned out for the meeting almost a hundred percent. They came afoot and in wagons. Very few owned cars. The men were dressed mostly in old blue overalls and the women wore faded, but clean, cotton dresses for the 'show' as they called it. The kids hung around in noisy, excited, little groups on the fringe, playing games, flirting, and challenging each other with insults, strength, and laughter.

Most of the grownups moved towards the wooden platform against the wagon. The nesters gathered into the largest group, while the ranchers clung together visiting and making nervous jokes.

Watching Duvall and the Apache place a heavy copper kettle on a fire in an iron grill, Rick said, "Well, the carnival's about to start. Wonder when the bearded lady and the two-headed calf'll be introduced."

Marta looked at him a moment to see if he really was joking, but she saw it was derision.

"It's not a carnival," she said, "it's a display of the power of medicine, just as you witnessed on the waterbelly steer."

"Here, here," Rick said, "I was only jokin'."

Marta turned from him, studying the movements of Duvall. The Apache started slowly beating a large Indian drum, almost in rhythm with Duvall's taking herbs and powder from some leather bags. He sprinkled some of each in the tub, moving his massive hands in a delicate rhythm to the slowly increasing throb of the drums. The crowd quieted and moved forward now. The children crowded close around the platform in front of the grownups or climbed on wagons to see better.

Now a young Apache woman came out of the wagon and started beating one of the drums in exact time with the male. The music picked up in tempo and the heads of the onlookers swayed in motion with Duvall's hands. Their eyes locked hypnotically on those powerful hands. He poured a bag of peyote into the steaming kettle, and, rising with hands held above his head and the palms towards the crowd, he said.

"The last powder completes the brew, my friends. It is an ancient one used for centuries by the Apaches and only now, here today, made available for all. Its powers to heal and soothe are from the body of Christ himself. It elates and quiets the tormented in a single swallow. It lifts you from the devil's depths to the glorious soaring heights of the gods of the rainbowed heavens. It takes you through doors of gold with windows of diamonds into a castle miles high. There, you'll hear," his voice increased measureably now, as did the drums, "the sweet voices of ten million angels lifted in eternal song. The fruits of all the many worlds will be stacked fresh, crisp, and delicious for your hungry tongues."

The hands of Duvall moved in slow circles now, and the breathing of all the audience was getting heavier.

"And there," he continued, "in silken cloth you'll lounge with velvet flesh, and feast and drink and love in a vast, limitless, golden sun, warm with seductiveness!"

The drums were at their peak now—speaking to, shifting, jerking, the nerves of all.

Marta stood staring, swaying, trembling. Her flesh seemed loosened from her bones with an enormous vibration of warmth. She heard Duvall pleading above the drums for the first to taste his nectar. Slowly she moved towards him, not feeling the tug of her husband's hand, seeing only the eyes and hands of Duvall.

She took the large gourd dipper and drank deeply of its hot fluid, never taking her eyes from Duvall. She could feel it slither down her throat and into her stomach and spread through her blood to the surface of her skin and behind her eyes and into the depths of her skull. And now she was sure she stood above the ground, floating in air so warm and softly caressing that her body flowed with all the juices of love.

Several of the large gourds were passed about and the drums pounded into the night and into the being of every one, just

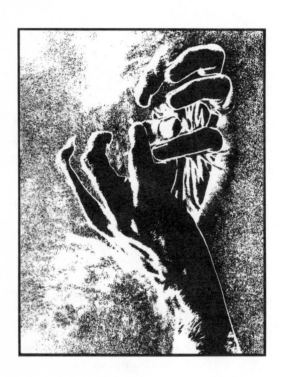

as the liquid did. And there was a sweating in the cool night as the fluid moved to the skin and the bodies began to jerk harder with the drums.

There was a murmur rising now, a slow, soft, communal voice of mass love. It rose slowly like the howl of a steady wind, and then it broke into pieces as the nesters began to pair off and move about dancing to the drums. Then some lay rolling on the ground as Duvall shouted into the night.

"Love, love, you heathens. Love and be complete! Heal all your aches and sorrows with the ecstasy of perfect, purified love."

Some of the ranchers left. Others stood, torn by it all.

Marta moved to Rick, slowly enveloping him in her arms. For a moment he took her almost desperately and then he pushed her away, grabbed her by one arm, and dragged her past the couples rolling on the ground and embracing against trees. A moaning came from them now, and Duvall screamed,

"Now, brothers, now. Talk to and embrace the gods!"

The gourds went the rounds among those still standing and moans and a loud shout of unintelligible words broke into the night. Shrieks of every kind rent the air like flashing swords as Duvall shouted over and over,

"Now, now, now!" His words were like the drums, like the shrieks; and all the air and all the earth and all the flesh became one, filled hot with rhythm and with lust.

Rick pulled Marta away from the sound even though she looked and struggled back towards it mutely, and with surprising strength. He finally got her to the truck. He could feel the drink still searing at his own inner body. He felt like a fool for partaking of it.

Marta crawled across the cab to him and he could not fend

her off. He drove with difficulty. Finally, he pulled from the road and took her to the ground and moved savagely into her quivering flesh. The sounds were soft in the distance now, like wolves howling in a far canyon.

You don't mean to tell me you're goin' back again?" Rick asked.

"Of course. It's a fine thing the Reverend Duvall is doing."

" A fine thing! God uh mighty, woman!"

"It's all free. It's the only relief those poor nesters have had in years."

"That's the whole damn problem, Marta. There's a catch to it somewhere. It just ain't natural for that Duvall to be givin' things away free. There's goin' to be a mighty big catch come to light. A mighty big one."

"All you ranchers are alike. You want all the land and power. When someone comes among you who doesn't care, and has something to give mankind, you just go blank and start cursing it."

"Well, the way he had those folks rollin' about on the ground, I ain't settled in my mind yet just what it is he has to give."

"Don't try to make something vulgar out of it. He's given those poor creatures love. They've found love again for the first time since you ranchers ran them off their land."

Rick pushed at his hair, scratched his head, got up and walked over to the stove to pour himself another cup of coffee.

"How long is Duvall intending to stay here in the Two Mesa country?"

"Just this summer," Marta said, looking at Rick with eyes that spoke only inwardly.

"Since he's been here, five weeks ain't it, you haven't tended to your chores worth a damn. Everything is just half-done. That ain't no way for a rancher's wife to carry on. It just ain't done, that's all. It don't pay. All these years we've been gainin' and all of a sudden we come to a standstill, all over some crazy preacher."

"No, Rick, that's not all. We've talked this over a *thousand* times, but you've never heard *once*. There's things a woman needs. Especially since she's helped earn them and there's money in the bank to buy them."

"Now, let's not go into that again."

"See, you close up every time. You can't face it. You can't face up to what's happening."

"All right, all right, if that's all that'll do you, just go on to the preachin' as long as the summer's a third over anyway. But this fall, early, it's goin' to be different. We're goin' back to actin' like we always have. You hear?"

"Oh yes, I hear you all right, Rick. How could I help it?" Marta turned to do the morning dishes.

Marcus had long since gone out to work on the hay stack fence. Rick got up, swallowed the last of the coffee, put the cup down hard, got his hat from the deer horns on the wall, jerked it down over his head, and clomped out. He walked down to see how Marcus was doing at the feed lot.

"Have eet finish by night, Reeck. We can start cutting hay mañana."

"Good." Rick looked down south to the sub-irrigated vega grass meadows. "Looks like we'll have a big first cuttin'."

"Si, the summer is a good wan for the grass."

"Well, we're due another hard winter. Comes every nine years for sure. Real bad ones, I mean. If a man's ready, lots can happen in his favor."

Marcus stopped a moment and looked at his boss, then silently went back to work stapling the wire on the newly set posts.

Rick said, still staring at the lush meadows, "I got to go work Brother Bill. He's getting a little soft."

But he went by the garden first and, taking a hoe where it leaned up against the fence, he dug the furrows so that all would water. He noticed that the beans were doing well as usual because of the early rains, but the rest of the garden—the tomatoes, carrots, and corn—all looked just a little wilted.

He took a piece of bent tin and put it sideways under the windmill spout. The water moved out into the garden soil. He could feel Marta's eyes on him from the kitchen window. This was her job and she knew it. It gave Rick a satisfaction that he couldn't define to do this chore in front of her.

Then he walked to the corral, caught and saddled the appaloosa. He reined him out across the lengthening gramma grass and rode down to his meadows. He had many stacks of old feed left, and he would add a lot of new to the reserve. The next time a blizzard struck he'd buy up a lot more of the cattle and the land. Feed would do it. Plenty of feed was money in more than one bank. A man had to see ahead and figure to make it out here in this weather-controlled land. Yes sir.

He felt a warm glow as he rode back out towards the foot-hills to the north. Might as well check out the bull pasture while he worked his horse. He kept a few high-blooded bulls here in a good, protected pasture. That was another way he was ahead of most of the ranchers, even those much bigger than he

—he kept improving the blood of his stock.

He was just leaning over to step down from Brother Bill and open the gate into the bull pasture when he sensed riders coming.

He turned and looked to the east and recognized three of his neighbors: George Randall, Scott Allen, and Moreno Cruz.

They rode up, all cattlemen, except Moreno who ran cows and sheep both. They got through the 'howdys' fairly quickly. Rick could tell they had something else on their minds.

George came right out with it first, "Rick, we was headin' over to see you."

"Yeah, what can I do for you, George?"

"It's like this, Rick. That Duvall is messin' up our country."

"How's that?" Rick asked, feeling cold in his spine and thinking of Marta who was probably driving the old truck into town right now for a meeting.

"Well, he's stirrin' up the nesters somethin' terrible. He's got 'em half drunk all the time on that free whiskey or whatever the hell it is."

Moreno Cruz pushed his black hat back from his kinky, grey hair and said, "It ain't really free. All during the week, the nesters have been bringin' gifts."

"Yeah, they're called love gifts," Scott Allen said, rolling a smoke of Prince Albert and pushing his hat back from his sad, horseface.

"The way it looks to us," Randall interrupted, "is the gifts are all for the love of Duvall. These nesters are bringin' him their canned goods, and some are even droppin' money on him. Others bring grain and early garden stuff. Duvall's been peddling this stuff in town at half wholesale. The merchants can't afford to turn it down, cuz he'd just haul it on over to Flagstaff."

"Well, whatcha want me to do about it?" Rick asked.

"Rick, at the risk of makin' you mad, I'm goin' to say this. All the ranchers have flat forbidden any of their kin to attend. They've all quit but Marta. Now the nesters kind of look up to her there. You know how it is. If she'd drop out of those meetin's and sort of pass the word around, we feel the nesters would get the message. They're goin' to wind up on the dole this winter if that Duvall keeps after 'em."

Moreno Cruz added, "Guess whose going to have to keep them from starving?"

"Well, I'll talk to Marta," Rick said stiffly, "But what she does is her business." He got down, opened the gate and rode into his bull pasture without another word.

His old friend Randall yelled after him, something he'd never done before in Rick's whole life, "Your old daddy would've recognized the fact he ain't no Reverend, Rick. He's some kind of a demon."

Rick rode on feeling an embarrassment, and a slow, infinitesimal wrath building deep down in his craw.

He rode slowly this day as he checked out and made a count of the bulls. Many things were on his mind. Many new emotions crossed the heavy, dedicated frame. He finally admitted to himself that he knew what to do about a cow or horse under any conditions, but this preacher business his wife was mixed up in was something else. He sure didn't want to lose her. He'd been a long time training her and preparing her for the big, acquisitive years ahead. It would be a hell of a loss. No, he couldn't just flatly forbid her to go. He'd already made his promise that she could attend until the end of the summer. There'd just have to be some other way. Maybe she'd tire of the hullabaloo, or maybe he could discreetly point out the

drawback and the consequent damage it was doing him among the other ranchers.

With all these thoughts twisting and undulating through his mind another message penetrated: one of the old bulls was missing.

He rode the fence awhile, then he came to the place where the wires were down. There the fresh, big tracks, much rounder than a cow's, had passed through. By the time he'd tracked the bull, driven him back to the pasture, and repaired the fence it was after dark.

The coyotes howled and sang at a three-quarter moon hanging in perpetual gravity, reflecting a soft blue light a quarter of a million miles through space to give voice to the coyote, light to lovers' eyes, and an easier path home for a rancher's tired horse.

As he rode, Rick's thoughts left the cattle and he wondered if Marta would be home when he got there. Then way below, near the ranch, he saw the lights of a vehicle moving to his house. No doubt that was Marta.

It took him another hour to wind around and enter the home pasture. Why didn't the old dog bark? He wondered about this as he unsaddled and fed his horse. Then he walked slowly towards the house. Out of the shadows of the hen house stepped the old dog. He moved up behind Rick, his bristles up, totally silent. There were no lights on in the house. No night birds voiced their approval of this mellow evening. Then he saw her. Marta stood on the porch in the moonrays. She was naked, and the blue lights caught at her breasts, caressed her round belly and outlined her dark head. She stood, arms upraised, stretching, swaying slightly like a grass stem in a small breeze. A noise came from her, not words, not moans, just a soft noise, almost like a cat purring, but smoother.

Rick was struck by the beauty, the symmetry, of the luscious, blue cast body, and he could not think logically.This was something he had no knowledge of, no answer for. He didn't even have a question.

He whispered softly, "Marta."

Her head came down from the sky and turned slowly to him. Her eyes were brighter in the moonlight than he'd ever seen them in the noon sun. She swayed from the porch towards him and he caught her smooth, naked body and stood shaking violently as she slowly, expertly took his shirt from him. She dropped it and he awkwardly and in desperation took the rest of his clothing off. Holding her feet just off the porch, her naked body tight against his own, he carried her into the house and dropped her on the rug in the living room where a shaft of moonlight stole through a window and drew a place on the floor for their lust.

She was wild and soft, mean and kind. She was a bitch mate to the coyote that howled again in the draw just in front of the house. She was mistress to the bobcat that prowled on the mesa a mile to the west. She lusted and whored for the brown bear in the mountains miles to the north and she was all of these and more for the man who moved grasping above her in abandon. Then everything became motionless, wet, and soft except the lungs. They too, finally subsided, and the woman slept.

Her husband carried her to bed and lay beside her where they both slept deep, deep down in rest and darkness. And the coyotes hunted on as the moon arced over until its light was destroyed by the orange heat of the rising sun.

Marcus, usually talkative and good-humored no matter what the labor in the pastures had taken in physical effort, ate breakfast in silence. Rick gulped his food and sat drinking coffee, looking out at the pastures without seeing them. Marta seemed almost normal, like she was before the coming of Duvall.

Finally Rick broke the silence, "Get the work horses harnessed and ready, Marcus. We might as well start cutting hay today."

Marcus gulped down the hot coffee, got up, and left. The two sat again. Marta waited. Rick cleared his throat. He got up and poured another cup of coffee. Suddenly he had to talk. It hurt to think of it. He told her of the conversation with the neighbors. She didn't speak, only looked at him with huge eyes that spoke not.

He said tensely, "I've promised you can go if he stays the summer, and I'll keep it, but don't you see or care about the position you're puttin' me in?"

Marta seemed to shrug off an invisible shroud. Her eyes had expression now, her nerves came alive, her whole body warmed and seemed to be quivering inside. She got up, went to the cupboard, and brought out an empty bottle. She set it in front of Rick. He stared at it.

"What's that for? It's empty."

"It wasn't empty last night on Salt River. I've invited the maker of its contents here tonight."

Rick felt that little tiny wrath swell in his belly and cord up into his chest and face. He leaped to his feet.

"You've invited that devil here, here to my house?"

"*Our* house, dear. Yes, he's coming this afternoon."

Ricked leaped at her and jerked her head sideways, violently, and there he held her off balance. "It's not enough that you go and make a fool of me with those goddamn nesters, is it? Well, he's not coming here. I'll kill the son of a bitch.Do you hear me? I'll kill the son of a bitch!"

"Let me go," she said, straining her whole body in the awkward position.

He flung her across the table. Things jarred and broke from the impact and Marta fell among them on the floor. He stood heaving, wanting to strike her and hurt her.

Calmly she got up and straightened herself. Then she opened her robe and he stared at her nakedness. She rubbed her hand across the smooth oval belly and said softly,

"You curse him and you curse his medicine, but now you have a son in here because of it." She patted the belly tenderly and an enigmatic smile formed on all her face.

A whole world of dark blue and charging, jumping, little pieces of lightning shot all around and through Rick's body. The knees ran together and helped each other to stand.

"You mean it? You mean it? You mean it?"

She moved to him, took his face, and kissed the repetition out of his mouth. Then she stepped back and said,

"Go to your work. You'll soon have many extra responsibilities. Many you don't dream of now."

The big man walked out to the team and in a little while he was following Marcus, doing what he knew how to do best. Marcus' team pulled the mower and the click, click of the blade made the world real again for Rick. He drove his team pulling the rake and dragging the cut hay into little windrows so it would be easy to load and stack later.

Now he'd have an heir and a helper and the ranchers could no longer taunt him. Oh, it was a great day! He smelled the

new-fallen hay and it smelled just as Marta had the night
before. He wanted to yell at Marcus the news and wonder of
the day, but somehow held it back. He failed to see the purple-
clad figure on a horse ride to his house and stay awhile and
then ride away.

After they finished the day's work and were turning the
horses to feed, Rick felt he must tell Marcus. Marcus had
shared in the labor for many steady years; he would rejoice
just as Rick had rejoiced about the son to come. But before
he could say anything Marcus himself spoke.

"Boss, I donn won to tell you thees, bot Terrasina the witch
tells me last Saturday in town for you to watch. Much evil is to
come unless you watch. Eet ees not my beezness, Boss, bot
watch."

"Watch what, Marcus?"

"She donn say what, Boss. She just say."

Rick walked towards the house. He could see the old dog
standing stiff, motionless, sniffing down the road towards town.

Marcus lifted the last fork of grass hay from
the wide bed wagon up on the stack. Rick finished rounding
out and tamping right the top of the stack. This would keep the
moisture out. He slid down one end and the two of them pulled
a strand of barbwire across the top of the stack and tied a
heavy rock to each end. This constant weight would hold the
stack solid and preserve it for several years if necessary.

Rick wiped the sweat from his head, taking his hat off to
cool a moment. The haying for the summer was finished. He
looked over row after row of stacks. He had more hay up now

than any three ranchers in the country. He was ready. It had to come. Either a bad drouth or a blizzard. They always did. In fact, it was very dry now. Although the gramma grass was up long, it had turned brown and matured early. In the fall, the cows would tromp down as much as they'd eat. Then if the blizzards came, Rick would sell the hay high and buy the cattle cheap. It was nothing new. You just had to save the dollars during the good times and get ready. Disaster had always struck the land, and Rick knew it always would.

He was also pleased that Marta had gone ahead with the garden and finished most of her canning. They would save lots of money on groceries this winter besides eating well.

It was mid-afternoon and a little hotter than usual for this time of late summer, and in mid-afternoon there was always more work to be done. But the thoughts of all the accomplishments made Rick suddenly generous with a little time.

"Marcus, you might as well take a nap, or plait on that rawhide bridle you been makin' for the youngun."

"Boss, maybe now you got the windmill turned on, you have much fruit. Huh?" Marcus grinned big. "That's the same way with me, Boss. I donn stop. Not ol' Marcus. I got another one comin' out of the same pot. Maria Sanchez. I donn open my eyes ever agin when we make the love."

"What's that got to do with it?"

"That's what makes the bambinos. I tell you, Boss, three times I open my eyes. Three times now the leetle ones. A man should not see so much in the world. No?"

Rick felt warm with the sun and thoughts of the new haystacks and the child in the lovely belly of his wife. He went to the house. She looked at him puzzled and said,

"Something wrong?" He never quit this early. Never.

"No, just thought I'd come visit a spell. The hayin's all done. We had a big crop. This last cuttin' was almost as good as the first. We're ready for 'em."

"That's good," she said flatly, and went on with her sewing. She was making new curtains for the living room.

"Rick, do you think we could have a new rug to match the curtains. This one's awfully old, and Allen's Hardware has a new assortment priced plenty reasonable."

"Well, let's wait and see how the calf crop weighs out. It's goin' to be a hard winter and you never can tell when a man might get in a tight."

Marta went on sewing silently. How could she penetrate through to this man? How in holy hell could she make him see something besides his fat cattle, his stacks of premeditated hay? She had helped make it all, including the bank account in town. She'd sewed, canned, dug in the garden, helped at brandings, cooked, skimped, done without, until now they were safe. What was it all for? She wanted what was normal — a car, a few new things for herself and the house. Not a lot, but some. And a little time in town to be sociable, to meet and talk and dream a little with other women. All this she ached to tell Rick. But her voice stopped and choked in her throat holding the emotions back with it.

Rick uneasily got up and poured himself a drink of bourbon. "Care for one?" he asked Marta.

She shook her head, and continued sewing.

He sipped a moment at the brown liquid and then belted it all down. He drank little. It was a luxury. He stared at the woman, thinking about the child in her hardening belly. He had her now. She hadn't insisted on the rug and caused a scene as she usually would. It was the kid. It had mellowed her. He wanted to make her feel how he felt. How it had been in the early days. How it was when his grandfather had come to Two Mesas with the first herd of cattle.

There had been a big gold-mining boom. The town had grown and pulled—with the magic word 'gold'—the miners, the merchants, the whores from all over the West. The mines had paid off for everyone for awhile. The town had been wild and mean and greedy. The boom crowded the mines, took the best ore out, ruined the tunnels, and then it died swiftly. The ghosts of people stayed and others moved on hunting the same elusive fortune, and their ghosts clung to the rotting buildings and to the wind whistling along the streets and through the windowless buildings.

Other cattlemen came. They settled right here. Lived on this land. Rick's grandfather spread out until he ran over two thousand head of cattle and it was a two-day ride across the land. The old man died and was buried on the little hill behind the house. Rick's father had taken over and spread out even bigger. Two Mesas grew and became a solid little cow town, serving its people well, supplying the extras—the salt and pepper of life.

But then, when Rick was a very small boy, he remembered the great blizzard and how the cattle vanished breathing the searing cold into their lungs and freezing their red hearts, and how finally the few left were moved to the stack lots and they tailed them up by the hour trying to save some for seed. His mother had stood there in the terrible cold working like a man. Then pneumonia had killed her just like the cattle. The tiny haystack had vanished and the cattle, too. They'd sold part of the land, and then some more, to hold together and restock. Finally things began to look good again, and Rick rode with his father; he had become a hand. Shortly thereafter the drouth came, and the wind lifted little bits of the earth from around the dying grass and everything became earth and dust — the sky, the insides of a man's head, his thoughts; even his dreams turned to dust. Once again he'd seen the hay dwindle and the cattle get down and breathe the dust like they had the iced air and die just the same. This last had killed his father. He just fell over dead one day.

Well, Rick took over the ranch as a very young man. How could he tell this feeling to Marta. He'd tried. She seemed to listen, but she'd never once said, 'I understand.'

He had learned a long and hard lesson and when the drouth hit in thirty four he'd been ready. All the good years before he'd put up hay. True he'd had to sell the ranch down to its present modest size but it was solid and it would grow again. *He'd* be buying up the land next time. It was his turn. Nothing could stop him. Nothing.

Marta sat looking at Rick now, as he stared out the window. She wondered what emotion made his jaw muscles knot and his breath come hard. Maybe he'd been thinking things over. Maybe she *should* approach him again about her desires.

"Rick," she said timidly. He turned to her. "Rick, I was just thinking about the new rug. We'll wait and see if the calves weigh out, but we both know they will. But in the meantime maybe I could have Mr. Allen put the rug back while I still have a good choice. There's a brown and red patterned one I want so bad."

Rick felt the flow of blood to his face. He leaped up. "*Want, want,* that's all you do is want. Can't you see what we're building for. If it's not a new car, it's a new rug. Why don't you have the Reverend Duvall buy you one. He's robbed the nesters until they'll all be on the dole this winter. It'll be the taxes we working people pay that'll be takin' care of 'em!"

Marta laid the sewing down in her lap and pushed her hair back. A color came into her cheeks as if they'd been freshly rouged. Her eyes and her nostrils widened measurably.

"Well, you can rest assured the Reverend knows when the old ways are done. He's selling his wagon and buying a new limousine in just two weeks. He knows the days of the horse-drawn show are over, but you don't, Rick. You'll die horseback on the way to the bank."

"Speakin' of the Reverend." Rick snapped short each word, "When is he going to finish up sacking out our country?"

"He'll finish two weeks from this Saturday and we're all going to miss him terribly."

"Well, I know a lot of people that won't."

At that instant the old dog barked for the first time in three months. Rick put on his hat and walked out to see what could have stirred the old critter up. Then he saw it! Down to the southwest a great line of blue and black smoke.

"Prairie fire!" he yelled, "Marta, it's movin' this way! The brooms!" he said, "get me all the brooms!" He raced to the corrals and got Brother Bill, then he rode to the house. Marta handed him the brooms from the kitchen door. He didn't tell her goodbye. He spurred to the bunkhouse where Marcus napped.

"Marcus! Marcus! Get up! There's a prairie fire! Get the plow, get the team, plow around the haystacks!"

He rode swiftly now, across the prairie towards the coming fire. Marta stood in the yard watching, breathing heavily, and the old dog just barked and barked as if he'd never bark again.

About a mile and a half from the front point of the fire, Rick saw his first bunch of deer. Several coyotes ran right among them. They were scattered, wildly leaping and running from the line of smoke and flame. Then he saw cattle rumbling ahead, slower, but just as frantic.

As he neared, he began to see the small things. Quail burst in frenzied rhythms across the sky. Rats dodged back and forth, some turning madly into the fire. Jack rabbits and cotton-tails seemed to lose direction and many of them leaped right into the flames, running, burning then falling in a kicking, smoking wad. A badger waddled ahead, side by side with a skunk, and there were all sorts of things moving, too small to see, lizards, scorpions, ants, grasshoppers, spiders, all roasted and turned black like the grass.

The wind was getting up from the southwest now as the sun set. All over the land people poured towards the battleline, in trucks, cars, wagons, and on horseback they came. Up and down the line they fought with brooms, shovels, raincoats, whatever they could throw at the fire.

Brother Bill was wild and scared of the fire, but Rick fought him under control. He got down with the brooms and moved in between several blackened, smoky men who were swinging various implements to smother the fire. They swung and fought and moved on. Finally Rick could see they weren't gaining any. The fire would be put out for a short distance then leap ahead to another point.

Darkness came and all up and down the line for two miles the black night figures flailed and struggled, and little pincers kept moving ahead with the wind.

If something desperate wasn't done, it would move on towards Rick's place, destroy it, and then take in Two Mesas itself. No doubt Salt River would be hit before it stopped.

Rick went back to get Brother Bill where he'd tied him to a tree. It took twenty minutes to walk back. He was amazed at how far the fire had run. He rode swiftly down the line. He could see where someone had attempted to plow in front of it, but the fire had simply run around. He saw Moreno Cruz and a group of ranchers trying to get a tractor ahead of the fire. Then two cowboys came racing down the line dragging a freshly butchered cowhide tied between two ropes. This checked the fire until the tractor could be moved out in front. But it didn't do any good. It was only a temporary relief. The cowhide dried swiftly; the rope burned in two.

Rick yelled at Moreno, "The only chance we got is to back-fire it."

"Can't as long as the wind is straight out of the southwest. It's changing a little, but not enough yet."

All over the land, women and small children stood in the yards of the ranches and looked at the red, mad glow flickering into the sky. Some had already seen their houses, barns, and fences go, cattle burn and run away in flames. The rest just stood waiting, praying and hurting with their men. The nesters' homes were safe because of the river, but they came and fought till they dropped or until some little dent was made in the line of destructive flame. All worked, hoped, and fought together now.

The man on the tractor kept trying, moving ahead, ripping at the untouched grass, and it did finally help. In his elation he forgot to watch and the fire crept up on the tractor. There was a loud explosion and another flame shot higher into the sky than any of the prairie fire. The tractor had caught fire and blown up. The flames were so hot that nothing could be done. The people of the land just fought on wearily around it.

The fire moved on. The main point now reached out within a mile and a quarter of Rick's southernmost pasture. He was sick all over. He called a conference with the ranchers.

"We've got to back-fire now!" he screamed into the night. "The wind is coming from the side now. There's a chance we can blunt the point. Moreno, you, Scott, Darby, Holzein scatter to the west and back-fire. I'll get a group and fight the main point."

But just as he gathered the men to him and rode, ran, and stumbled for the blazing, searing front point, the wind increased and shot the flames higher and faster ahead. They fought hard and many were burned, but the anxious wind would not listen as it hurried, crowded, and shoved the fire forward where it licked and devoured all life ahead of it.

Then there was a loud rumble and Rick looked to see the white canvas of a wagon hurtling along the fire line towards them. It came to a halt so suddenly that the wagon almost overturned and the horses were nearly jerked from the harness. It was Duvall's Apache at the reins and beside him, horseback, rode Duvall himself.

He alighted like a calf roper from the horse, handed the reins to the Indian and yelled. "Here, help!"

Rick ran to him and helped drop a barrel from the back of the wagon into the burnt earth.

"Get your horse," Duvall yelled, and with huge hands he jerked an iron loop from the barrel and ripped a canvas cover from its top.

Rick ran back for Brother Bill not knowing why he obeyed. He spurred back and Duvall dragged a huge buffalo hide out of the barrel of dark liquid.

"Here," he shouted, "dip your rope in here."

Rick pitched the rope to him and dipped it in. Duvall had already dipped his. Swiftly the mighty hands tied the ropes on opposite sides of the hide. Rick didn't have to be told what to do. He and Duvall mounted and dallied their ropes around the horns of their saddles. He could tell by the expert and practiced way Duvall did this that he'd worked with the California vaqueros at one time. They split now on each side of the fire and rode. Oh, how they rode!

Brother Bill sensed a job to do now. This was what Rick had trained him for—to be ready for any job and to handle it. They rode and dragged the hide. As it hit the flame great phosphorescent lights ricochetted out from it like little concentrated bits of moonlight, and the fire died. They spurred back to the barrel, dipped the hide, and rode wildly again into the night.

The horses were heaving and sweating and their hair became singed. The lungs of the men filled with smoke and the whites of their eyes turned red and profane like the prairie fire itself. But all held together. They broke the point of the fire, and then dulled it more and there was a great gap where it was dead. Then the back-fire met the main line and the two points fought themselves out of flame and into smoke and died together.

Now the people of the land sensed victory and they struck at the tiny little outbreaks. Soon the line was only black and smoking.

As the sun came up the people stayed. Back behind, things still smoked, carcasses, dry cow dung, and lumps of things, but on the front line itself all had been pounded out.

Duvall was gone. He'd taken the hide with him. The people left one by one.

Rick, a half mile from his land now, could see the gate standing up. It stood erect, steady and unburned. And the dry, rich grass still waved in the now-soft wind across his land. His haystacks were still there to serve his purposes. And in the house his wife with the beautiful belly surrounding a child from his loins would be there waiting.

He rode the tired horse across the black, weaving fire-line that caressed the brown, waving grassy one, towards his world. He hadn't even had a chance to thank Duvall. Everyone had been too busy. Well, he'd do that, and he'd tell Marta how wrong he'd been. But by the time he rode past the haystacks to the house a part of this vow had slipped his mind.

Marcus stood waiting where he'd plowed all night long around the stacks. And the old dog stood with bristles up and he was silent again.

With the saving of the land from the devouring fire, a new fear came over Rick. He could not say what this fear was exactly. He *felt* like the old dog *looked*; that was as close as he could come to it.

It was the last night of Reverend Duvall's meetings. He didn't want Marta to go. Still he knew she would. Everyone in the country knew that it was a healing and marrying night. He was afraid of this night.

Suddenly he said to Marta, "I'm going with you."

The hand holding the brush that caressed her hair stopped its motion for an instant only, "All right. It's about time," she said, in that voice that spoke only words.

He tried to watch her as the old truck bumped along. But

the huge eyes had a film over them that he could not penetrate. His uneasiness increased as they neared town.

"Do we need anything from Allen's?" he asked, and then wished he hadn't as he remembered the rug she wanted.

"No, we don't need anything."

"Would you like a cup of coffee?" he asked.

"I guess so."

They walked in Lil's place just as several cowboys they knew were getting up to leave.

"Howdy, Rick," They all said. None of them spoke to Marta. Rick noticed this but couldn't define it. Lil came over saying,

"I hear you just missed burning out, Rick."

"Yeah, it was close."

"They're telling around that Reverend what's-his-name saved the day."

"He helped," Rick said. "Coffee, Lil, and I'll take some of that peach cobbler of yours."

Lil looked at Marta, waiting.

Marta said, "Just for the fun of it I'll take the same as Rick." She looked up at Lil and smiled. Lil looked away, then went to get the order.

They were silent until it was delivered. Lil went straight back to the kitchen saying over her shoulder,

"If you need anything just holler. I've got some chores to do in the kitchen."

Rick could feel a certain coldness all around them. It was like seeing a warm pond turn to ice on a sweating hot day. It made no sense to him. He felt alone.

Marta studied Rick now. She thought, he just doesn't get it. He's forgotten that I gave up a fine life in California for him.

If nothing else I could be living with my parents who are well-to-do merchants. I could have had the pick of the men in Fresno. How did I go wrong? Where did I misjudge this man? Then she recalled it was his dedicated talk of power and wealth regained that had sold her in the first place. But, God, what was it all for? Just to have it was nothing. It was only the use it was put to that counted. She'd done her part, of that she was certain.

Rick looked at her and saw nothing but a beautiful statue with her arms folded across the growing and fertile belly. He strained. He tried to open himself to her feelings, but nothing came through. It was like a broadcast station with no receivers. He was like a hunting hound with nothing to scent. The air became static and a vacuum of opposites. They sat, these two persons, feeling much, knowing much, but her emotions bounced from the south wall and his from the north.

    The nesters came to the wagon in little groups and couples. They came to the magnetic core of something that gave a fleeting time of escape to them. It was different. It was a release and a relief from the grinding poverty and and indignity of their surroundings. For a time now they had felt big, even as big as the ranchers and the vast land that destroyed them. .

For the children it had been a dream. Never before had their parents been as free with them. Never before had they been as generous with the pitiful supplies of food. And instead of the constant petty bickering before Duvall came, there was now a semblance of loving and being loved.

And the word had spread, the story told and retold—of his stopping the prairie fire with another magical brew. This, the last night, saw the people of the little river come almost in awe. They were not rowdy as before, but restrained, anticipating a last great event, yet fearful of its outcome.

Rick and Marta stood watching the 'love offerings' placed in a large pile. They could see the steam already coming out of the pot, but Duvall and the Indians were still in the wagon.

One old man, obviously hooked on either Duvall's medicine or a concoction of his own, slithered up to Rick and smiled a toothless smile, twisting his hands in his overall pockets.

"Well, it's good to see you here, Mr. Ames. The missus has kept us real good company. Real good." And he laughed in a screaming, choking laugh that made Rick want to smash the old man in the face.

He controlled himself, not wanting these nesters to get the best of him in any way. He realized a rancher could lose face for years that way. What was the matter with him? He was not under his usual rock-like control.

Suddenly the Apache and his sister leaped up on the platform and moved to the drums. The crowd closed around now like gamblers at a cock fight. Slowly the drums started. The Indians played, looking out above the crowd. They only participated with the primitive beat. Their faces appeared made of red clay, fired, and set forever in the vacant look of *nothing*, or maybe *all* . . .

Then there was Duvall, his hands up, seeming to hide his husky body with their spread.

"Friends," he said softly, glancing slowly all through the crowd, lingering a moment on Rick and Marta. "Friends," and the black eyes seemed to have little electric bulbs in them, and a smile pulled one side of his face. "This will be our last glorious night together."

"No, no," came a couple of protesting voices from the crowd and then a chant rose, "No, no."

The hands moved slightly and the chant died. "Thank you, but other lands call us. We have done extraordinarily well here. We have given rise to old, long dead emotions and we have created an atmosphere of pure love. Love," the voice raised imperceptibly, "Love, and now tonight we'll consummate those loves among the young of marrying temperament, and we'll heal all the lame and halt. All! Do you hear, my brothers?"

"Yes," came the loud chorus back.

"Good. Ah excellent. I feel this is going to be one of our greatest nights. I've traveled all the world gathering the know-ledge of the ancients. It must not be wasted. That would be an unredeemable sin. Right brothers?"

"Yes, yes," they yelled. "Yes!"

Now the drums picked up gradually but definitely. The hands moved in tiny little circles.

"I ask you, my brothers, to come forward and bring your ill, and weak, and worried. Come to me." The hands moved out above the crowd and he drew all he mentioned with a motion of the hands.

They came now, the arthritic, the rheumatic, those with sinus and heart diseases, and those who were just old. There was one idiot who had been born an idiot and was now a fifty-seven-year-old baby. They led him like a mule and every-one now stood waiting in a single line, looking around the ones in front of them, waiting for Duvall.

Suddenly he leaped from the platform with a large gourd. He passed it down the line of sick.

"Drink, my brothers, drink and feel the blood purified, and the soul soothed like a baby at a sweet teat."

They drank the hot liquid, swallowed it down until tears swamped their eyes.

First in line was an old man on homemade crutches who couldn't stand alone. His wife helped him forward. The wife looked aglow with a fervor that Rick had seen only here, now, and the night he'd loved Marta in the moonlight. She held the old man as if Duvall would turn him into a golden everlasting statue.

Duvall swept his hands swiftly back and forth through the air above the old man and said, "Now, brother, what's your trouble?"

The woman said, "Arthritis, sir. He's had it nigh onto twenty years now. He ain't able to sleep er nothin' fer hit."

"Well, dear lady, hold this old crippled man. Hold him tight because he might just run off with a young widow in just one minute." The crowd laughed nervously but with a building excitement. "Old man, you want to be well?" The old man nodded *yes*, grinning like a fool. "Well, you are," Duvall screamed, leaping off the ground and waving his hands in powerful, swift arcs. "You're well," and he grabbed him by each shoulder . . . "You are healed! You are cured! You are FREE!" and he jerked the crutches from the old man and threw them out of sight into the night brush. "Dance", he screamed at him, and the old man, fearful at first, took a tender step. A strange, unreal expression came over his face and he did dance. His fat wife cried and screamed, and now all the crowd picked it up.

The voice of Duvall shafted through the mighty fingers and the words 'heal' and 'cure' and 'free' rent the skulls of all in line. All there. People moaned and prayed and thanked God and Duvall. They cried and fell and danced and vibrated to the tune of his voice, and the wild Indian drums were like balloons above a powerful fan. No one was ill anymore. They brought out their bottles like beggars, holding them forward to Duvall. The Indian woman quit the drum and helped fill them.

Rick stood, laying his hand on the quivering arm of Marta. He could feel vibrations running through her as if a mighty wind full of ice had blown her naked. He could feel some of this chill in his own blood and he fought at it, and was ashamed. Yet he stood transfixed. It was the last night, and he'd promised.

Then Marta took a bottle out of her purse and held it to Duvall who bowed slightly and filled it for her. She brought it back and handed it to Rick. He shook his head *no* and she shrugged, pulling deeply at the fiery liquid.

Now the bottles were filled and Duvall leaped on the platform again raising the hands. All heads and eyes moved up with them and stayed there moving to the side or down only as the hands did.

"Now, my brothers, the healing is done. You have been cleansed of the devil's curse and the gods are smiling on your blood. Ah, red, red blood, pure as high-country snow, warm as love, young love. All is blood, my brothers. All is blood. Come drink now and warm that blood and let it know life is there circulating, crying to break out of the prison of your ribs. Pour your life out to each other. You have an abundance of life tonight, my brothers. Pour it and revive! Now, now is the moment! All the young, the marrying young come here. Come, come." And again the hands made the wide, powerful gathering motion and the young came and stood in heat, the heat of the drink, of the voice, and the natural heat of stimulated youth, and he married them.

"Now, you are man and wife. Act! Act! Love! Be what you were born to be! You were born out of love. Now live from it. Give love. Receive!"

The vibration of the drums and the voice filled everything. There was not a single atom of the air that was not propelled by it. It came out of the earth, and the bodies that breathed the air and stood on that earth absorbed it and emanated it and the young fell into each others arms and they moved in the grass. All the unknown tongues of lost civilizations returned and entered these bodies as they talked, grunted, and fell about writhing. Some lost their new mates and found others and all were one single mind to Duvall's hands.

Rick looked in wonder at first; then the cannibalistic, hog-like noises nauseated him, and he felt the slow anger that burned like a coal stove flame stoked slightly. He saw Duvall's hands reaching toward them in the sky. He shook his head and almost fell. He wanted to sleep, but refused it. He willed it not to be. Then he saw Marta's face upturned, filled with the look of every captive woman who ever lived, every woman who was sold, conned, and deceived since the beginning.

Marta moved towards Duvall looking up at the hands, and now he looked down at her and spoke softly, "Come. Come."

The Apaches no longer played. The noise of the earth was not of the drums, now, but of mating tigers and hyenas.

Rick leaped at Marta, grabbed her around the waist, and started with her to the truck, and then it was all gone. There was one stab of pencil-straight lightning that shot like a comet into his universe and disappeared leaving nothing but the darkness.

It was still dark when Rick awakened. The bed was hard to ride. It whirled about and his head pained. He reached to feel the knot and the gash on the back side of his head. It still throbbed. It must have been the Apache. Duvall could never have reached him that quickly. He lay awhile and then he heard Marcus in the kitchen.

Daylight came, cool and grey through the bedroom window. Marta lay now with a peaceful look on her face. She always awoke when he did and fixed breakfast for the three of them. This morning she slept sounder than she'd ever done before.

He decided to leave her be. He put on his pants and bent to pull on his boots. The blood pounded in his head and he almost fell. By the time he'd dressed and walked to the kitchen he could feel the rage churning about through his being. He looked at the 30-30 above the door. Then he flexed his hands and thought of Duvall's throat.

Marcus sat drinking coffee. "Mornin', Boss. I kept the team up und they ready."

"What for?"

"To help feenesh Randall's tank. Donn you remember? We promise lass week."

"Oh hell, that's right. Well, we'll just have to go."

Rick poured himself a cup of coffee. Then took a side of bacon and sliced some. He fried them two eggs apiece. The sourdough bread baked quickly in the hot oven. They ate in silence.

Rick decided he had to give Duvall a whipping. There was no other way, but he couldn't go back on his word to help a neighbor. No telling when he'd need that help himself. Randall had broken a leg last week when a horse fell on him. The tank would dam up a long draw near Randall's headquarters. It was government-financed so Randall would draw wages for all his work. According to the government it was a way of helping the ranchers to overcome the drouth and recent depression, and at the same time improve the land.

Well maybe Duvall would stay a few days longer, to cash in his love offerings. If he did they had to have it out, that was all. Duvall had it coming, but even more Rick needed to give it to him.

They cleaned their plates with home-canned strawberry jam and hot, buttered sourdough biscuits. After a final cup of coffee, Marcus walked out and Rick looked for his hat. He always threw it on the deer horns in the kitchen, but it wasn't there. He found it by the bed. He could see the dent where he'd been hit with a hard object. He pulled it over his sore head and started out.

Then Marta's voice stopped him at the door. "When will you be back?" She spoke in the flat tones she'd used lately.

"Two and a half or three days, I reckon. Why?"

There was no answer. He left.

Marcus had the horses all harnessed and leaped up on one bareback. Rick rode Red Spot, a three-year-old gelding appa-loosa that would someday be as good a horse as Brother Bill. The horse moved out under him with the good running walk he liked. It helped his feelings. He rode beside Marcus, wonder-ing why he was silent. Everything seemed against nature lately. Then he noticed the old dog following lamely. He reined up and yelled,

"Go home you old fool. What's the matter with you?" The old dog stood and watched him until he moved ahead, then he followed again. The third time Rick took his rope from the saddle and shook it at the old dog. "Now, get on back."

To Marcus he said. "That old dog ain't tried to follow me in two years. Hell, he cain't hardly walk." The old dog refused to be cowed, but stopped and stood immobile, watching as they rode away.

Rick thought, *Why in hell doesn't Marcus comment?* The world he had regulated, cornered, and so efficiently controlled was suddenly deserting him. It was the helplessness he felt that brought on the rage. He had to do something just as soon as he finished Randall's tank. A move to stop all this must be made. He would damn well do it.

Now the sun came up over the two mesas that gave the town its name. It radiated out in oranges and yellows and the beams topped the grass in golden waves, warming the earth like hind-quarters against a fast burning fireplace. The blue jays whipped about swishing a little of the vast sky color among the deep green of the scrub-cedars. The coyotes and bobcats had gone to bed now, and the deer were hiding in little sunlit parks. The air was pure and quiet with a hint of the coming fall as it passed into the lungs.

Rick's feelings improved again as he saw a bunch of his cattle lying fat and full. The calves stood about, some jumping and running, full of the life and fat that meant money and power. He still wondered why Marcus was so silent. He was sure a good hand. He'd groomed him a long time now in every phase of ranch life from the doctoring of cattle to the cutting and stacking of hay. He had dug post holes, built fence, topped off a bronc, pulled calves from dying mothers, tailed up old cows in blizzards, broken ice for stock water in the winter, and hauled feed when the snow was two-feet deep on the level. Marcus was an all-around hand. Soon now the ranch would grow and demand more help. Marcus was to be the foreman.

Hell yes. The years had not been wasted, not if he held things together as before. But . . . but . . . .

Marcus sensed his boss, knew there was turmoil in his soul. He feared to approach him about it, having always been gentleman enough not to infringe on the other man's privacy. And yet, he felt a great urge to comfort him. Maybe the boss suffered some of the confusion that he felt within himself. Things were not the same anymore. He had heard his boss called a tight-fisted, greedy, grasping rancher many times. He knew better. Rick had always worked him hard, paid and fed him well—and he even allowed for his weekend drunks with understanding. He could not imagine being treated better. And Marta, too, had given him respect and a place at their table. He could not conceive living without the two of them. But now something threatened his home, his life, his dedication. Something that Terrasina the witch had consistently warned him about. But he could not approach his boss from that angle. It was too delicate, and the results too fearful. Still he *had* to cheer him up. He would think of something to make him feel better.

"Boss, when you get your leetle one, I goin' to borrow him and take him to see all three of mine. Donn you think they'd like that? Who knows, Boss, maybe someday your son marry with my gurrl. Huh?"

Rick said, "Might be. A feller never knows what's goin' to happen these days."

"Boss, I aver tells you about thees time I wins seven hondred dollar in a game of the dice?"

"No."

"Well, the dice talk altogether for ol' Marcus. They says over und over seven, seven, seven. Booms, booms, booms.

All the time I take the money an' put een my pockets. Pretty soon I ron out uv pockets and so I queets the game. I go across the streets to another bar. There is poker game. I get in the poker game and thees man he give me all thees cards, and all thees whiskey I'm buying for ourselves. Preety soons I donn know if I got aces or deuces. Then I bat it all. All in wan pot. I know wat you goin' to theenks, Boss, bot you theenks wrong. I ween'! I tell you I weens eet all! I donn have enough pockets so I poot eet in my hat. Then I hire me one cowboy to drive me to Flagstaff and there I meet a girl een this place. She say she ees married bot her hosbond donn be in town. Well, I buy wheesky, jeen, beers, und the wines. I go to spend time with thees pretty woman." Marcus looked hard at Rick and thought he sensed a slightly different feeling coming from his boss now. "Und, Boss, I stay, I donn know, maybe wan hour, maybe wan day. Then this man breaks up the door with muscles. He ees yelling noises at me. I jomp op and ron like hell. I geet plomb away that ees for chure. Bot, I donn got no pants. And that ees how I got broke on the dice games. Boss, donn never poot no money in your pants. Huh? Spend it on the bar and you donn lose nothin'. Huh?"

Rick grinned and said, "I'll try to remember that the next time I'm in Flag. By the way when's the last time you were in Flagstaff, Marcus?"

"Never no mores, Boss. The welcome she ees gone, gone."

Now they came to the tank. There was the slip or steel fresno as it was sometimes called. Marcus hitched the team to it and Rick tied his horse and took the reins. They went to work. The sun seared down and the dust came and choked them, filled their eyes, got under their collars, and mixed with the sweat trickling from under their hats.

Randall was soon there, driving up in his old pickup to bring them lunch. Randall got out of the pickup holding back with the leg that was in a cast.

He yelled, "You fellers like somethin' to eat?" and added, "I didn't really expect you to be here."

Rick said, "Did Sybil break that leg so she could keep you home awhile?"

"Hell, I ain't been anywhere but your place and mine in a month. I ain't goin' around Two Mesas till that Duvall is gone."

There was a silence now. Rick felt the anger come back, twisting around hot and bitter, wanting out, craving release.

They all sat down in the shade of the pickup. Rick took the bacon sandwich from the box and said, "Well, get it off your chest, George. You ain't let me alone since that bastard's been in the country."

"Well, I might as well get it over with like you say. Seeing as how your daddy and me was the closest friends in the country, it sorta hurt me to see you lettin' Marta go to them damn meetin's. You know I don't give a damn about gossip, but everyone in the country is talking about it. It could hurt you later on, Rick."

Marcus chewed nervously at his sandwich, not tasting it now.

"I know you're right, George, but there's things you don't know."

"Well, out with it, boy. Since I'm goin' to nose in my neighbor's business I might as well know it all."

"Well, it's like this. Marta's pregnant and I thought since it'd been so long comin' about I'd just humor her."

"Pregnant! Good Lord, boy, how come you didn't jist up

and tell me? Hells Bells!'' Randall leaped up forgetting about his broken leg and crawled across the pickup seat to the glove compartment. "Here," he said jerking out a quart of very brown whiskey, "Here, by God, we got to have a little toast to that."

Rick said, smiling, feeling another form of warmness and pride now, "Here's to the future governor of the state."

Marcus took a slug, feeling silly and happy again for the first time in a long spell. "Here's to the son of the Boss. We hopes he makes half as good as the papa and mama."

Randall took two swallows before he let the bottle down. He wiped his mouth and the tears from his eyes, and said, "If he turns into a first-class bank robber we'll toast him again, but if he's a petty thief we'll all help hang him."

They all yelled.

Some time later, after the sandwiches and the bottle were finished, Randall took a nap and his two neighbors worked like four mules. The tank was almost done when sundown came. They woke up Randall who was embarrassed at his being caught asleep at that time of day. He said,

"Hell of a note ain't it? Got my neighbors over here doin' my government work for me, then I drink most of the whiskey to celebrate the new son. Don't look like to me you boys 'er getting a fair deal out of this."

"I wouldn't trade places with you for a new set of harness," Rick said. "Besides Sybil will have some of that tongue-melting peach cobbler for supper. That'll even us up for a whole month."

After the horses were watered and fed, the men retired to the ranch house. Sybil and George ran it all now, except during

haying season. Their two sons were off in California somewhere, bumming around as George said, just wasting time till
they came back to the ranch. Sybil was one of those women,
tough and tender, strong-armed and flexible-backed—tight jaws
below smiling eyes. You knew that if she'd been raised in
society she'd have been its queen. And since it was a cow
ranch instead, she was the queen of the ranch. There was no
other word that fit her.

"How's Marta?" were her first words to Rick and there was
none of the questing and accusation he had heard in other's
voices when they asked him that. She really meant it, and
paid no mind to other's thoughts, figuring she was capable of
having plenty of her own.

"Oh, she's just fine, Sybil. Finished her cannin'. Had lots
of strawberries this year."

"Now wait a minute, Rick," said Randall, "tell her how she
really is."

Rick hung his head and felt he was blushing through the
seat of his levis.

"They're goin' to colt this winter," Randall said, watching
the joy spread over Sybil's face.

"Well, my goodness," she said, "that calls for somethin'
special." She went to a cupboard and pulled out a gallon jar
of homemade chokecherry wine.

Since this was Marcus' favorite drink in the whole world
he just stood there in the middle of the floor like he was going
to fly out over the windmill, and tried to rub the kinky hair
out of his head while he waited for his glass.

They all toasted the new one again and again. The kitchen
warmed up from the stove, the wine, the friendship, and joy
of a newcomer to an old, old world. Then Sybil cooked the

venison steak and hot biscuits and gravy that steamed and scented up the whole place. They all sat down and ate four bellies' full. Then, the now slightly cooled peach cobbler was dipped out with an extra portion for Rick.

"The new papa'll need a lot of extra strength from here on in," Sybil said.

They all slept that night full and happy. Yes, even Marcus and Rick felt that things were right again.

Rick and Marcus were up, breakfasted, and at the tank right after sunrise. By ten o'clock that morning the wind was getting up, but all the fresnoing was done. Rick took a shovel and helped Marcus tamp the tank awhile. Then they were done.

Rick smiled, "We did it, Marcus. She's finished. Ol' George can collect his money from the government and sweat out the spring rains from now on. Listen, you head on in home with the team, Marta isn't expectin' us back till tomorrow night, so tell her I'm helping George move some cattle. I want to go by the ranch and visit awhile with George and then drift on by Two Mesas and get a little surprise for Marta."

The wind blasted the dust from the freshly moved earth around them.

"Hell, let's get out of here," he said. They left.

Rick stopped and tied Red Spot and got in out of the wind. Sybil poured a cup of hot coffee for Rick and George who sat with his busted leg propped up on a chair.

"It's done, George."

"You fellers worked like you owned the place. I wasn't

expectin' this for two or three more days."

"It was that chokecherry wine of Sybil's."

"If I thought it'd make you men work like that all the time, I'd keep a batch brewin' day and night," she said.

"Say, Sybil," Rick asked, "what's Marta's favorite color?"

"You mean you don't know?"

"Naw."

"You're just like George. Everything that I bought in this house is blue, and the last time he bought me a dress it was red. You men."

"That's the reason I'm askin'. I thought I'd ride over by town and get her a new dress at Berg's."

"In that case, I'll tell you. She likes yellow best of all."

"I'll be damned. I'd have bought your color—blue."

"See, you men ought to pay more attention."

George said, "I still like red on Sybil."

The men had two more cups of coffee and talked of the coming child, the Randall's sons, and cows.

Rick said, "I better get goin'. I just hate to make that ride in this damned wind. I reckon I'm gettin' old."

He rode across the rolling prairie feeling the relentless force pull at his hat and watched the horse's mane and tail flip out and back in ceaseless motion.

In the Absolute Saloon in Two Mesas at just the time Rick and Marcus finished the tank, two cowboys who had been on an all night drunk were trying to cure their hangovers and were getting the job done. They worked for Scott

Allen, but had taken a little time off just before fall roundup and shipping came along.

One, Ellis Carter, a big, heavy-bellied, but lean-faced cowboy said, "Now, I'm tellin' you, Tiny," his pardner was huge all over, "we never had much fun last night. Here, bartender, give us another. As I was sayin' we never had much fun 'cause we never got in jail, a poker game, or no fist fights."

Tiny Sands answered, pushing his hat back from his red, corrugated face. "By god, you're right. We didn't even try to find any of the town whores."

Ellis added, "That's right, we just got drunk. Just plain ol' drunk and told a bunch of lies. I remember one thing you said. That if that Duvall stepped foot in town you was goin' to whup hell out of him."

Tiny blinked and finished the straight shot of bourbon, "I said that?"

"Yeah."

"What else did I say?"

"You said that he was tryin' to make a run at Rick's wife and that he'd messed up the whole country by breaking the nesters so all us cow people'd have to winter 'em or they'd starve."

"I said all that, out loud?"

"Yeah."

"Give us another'n, bartender. Now, Ellis, don't you go puttin' me on. Now, sure 'nough did I make all them comments . . . . 'bout . . . ." The two cowhands emptied another shot glass, wiping their mouths. ". . . bout that Duvall?"

"Yeah."

"I sure 'nough said I was goin' to whup him?"

"Yeah."

"Well then, I reckon I better get after it. There the son of a bitch goes to his new car."

Duvall strolled across the street to the new Dodge. He'd decided the horse and wagon days were over for Healers. From now on he intended to work out of school auditoriums, local theaters, and such. The Dodge and trailer would get him there. It would speed things up and pay much faster. He'd done well here though. He stuck the big roll of money from the 'love offerings' in his pocket when he heard the voice of Tiny Sands.

"Duvall!"

He stopped and waited silently, as the large cowboy loomed towards him followed by another. He could see Mr. Allen looking out the window of his hardware store and he took a quick look at the general mercantile. Nobody else seemed to be on the street. He'd been in this same spot before in other lands.

Tiny could see that they had him cut off from his car. He moved on to him and said softly, "Mr. Duvall, you ain't leavin' town?"

"Yes, tonight."

"How about right now."

"I'm not through packing."

"Well, pack this off with you," Tiny said, and swung a heavy vicious blow through the wind at Duvall's face. The face wasn't there. Tiny felt himself leaving the ground as Duvall caught his momentum and hurled him sideways and down. Tiny was almost up but still off balance when Duvall's hand came slapping into his Adam's apple. All the wind vanished from Tiny's body. He grabbed at his throat and the world turned as purple as Duvall's preaching clothes. Duvall jerked him up and let go with the other hand, the right and most powerful one, to the side of Tiny's jaw. It snapped and broke like a dead pine twig, and Tiny collapsed in a large pile of helplessness.

Ellis had fished quickly for a knife and he snapped the three inch blade open. Now a crowd came upon the sidewalks, a small crowd, but mysteriously, suddenly there—but no one moved into the street.

Ellis stalked forward toward the waiting, crouching Duvall. "I'm goin' to skin you alive for doin' that to my friend." He slashed at Duvall's chest, and missed a foot as Duvall slipped swiftly aside. Ellis looked at the two hands up in front of him now. It seemed they completely covered the body of Duvall. He could see the dark eyes peering straight at him through the widespread fingers.

He moved forward. Duvall was saying something in a low humming voice, but he didn't hear the words. *Hell, he'd just cut those hands off.* He slashed and missed and saw the hands move and circle and heard the humming again and suddenly all he could see were the beaming eyes and he cut at them and cut again as they danced away.

Then Duvall came at him swiftly, but Ellis didn't move until far too late. Duvall took his elbow in one hand and in the other he took the hand with the knife in it and drove it into the inverted V of Ellis' front ribs and upwards. It expertly split the main artery and plunged into the heart, and Duvall hurled him away and down dead, before the spewing redness could splatter a drop on him.

It was useless for the people of Two Mesa to call the sheriff. He was already there at the tail end of the fight. It was self defense. But an enormous feeling of loathing and hate had risen up in the town and was soon spread by phone and some other unknown manner across the lonely land. But Rick had already mounted to ride towards this tragedy without knowing or feeling it. He was thinking of Marta and a new dress for her sweet body. She would be too big to wear it in another six weeks, but she would have it to look at and to touch.

He felt a strange warmth surge around in him where there had been hot anger the day before. From now on he was going to do more for her. And he made a firm promise to himself that if the calves weighed out at four hundred pounds this fall he'd get the new car for her. He couldn't wait to tell her.

At this moment Ellis Carter was turning cold and Duvall was driving the new car towards the Ames' ranch.

Several hours later Rick tied Red Spot in front of Berg's Dry Goods. He didn't feel the town, but they all knew he'd just ridden in.

Mr. Berg said, "Hello Rick, it was terrible wasn't it?"

"What's that?"

"The killing."

"The killin'?"

"Yes, didn't you hear? Duvall killed Ellis Carter."

"Ellis? God uh mighty, Ellis is a good friend of mine. How'd it happen?"

"With a knife. With Ellis' own knife."

"Have they got the bastard in jail?"

"No," and then Mr. Berg described the whole thing to Rick.

A sick, painful feeling hit Rick, as if he had a belly full of stinging ants. He shook his head numbly. "That's too bad, just too damn bad." The urge struck him to get Duvall and tear him in little shreds and feed them to the magpies and coyotes. This same feeling was on most of the land. But there was also this one of helplessness, and it too came over Rick. "Well, I came after a new dress for Marta, Berg, and I aim to get it for her."

Berg showed him the yellow one she'd admired, "I know that's her favorite color."

"Yeah."

"And she liked this dress. It's rather expensive. That's the reason we still have it."

"To hell with the expense, wrap it up."

Rick rode out of town with the dress tied in a flat box on the back of the saddle. He soon forgot it. Wanting now to tell Marta about Ellis. Wanting to shove the knife of words into her about Duvall. He almost broke the horse into a lope — something he never did when heading home. It was the wrong thing with a horse. It would get so that's all they thought about was getting to the feed barn. But Rick also wanted time. Time to sort out in his mind all the things that had happened in the past hours, days. He cut across country, slowly, away from the winding road—or he might have noticed the tracks of a car in the road. His eyes had many other visions dancing along before them today.

He was home. He stepped down, tied the horse to the garden fence—then he saw it. The old dog in the yard. Dead. There was no question about it. He lay with the wind stirring the hair on his back just as some unspoken fear had all summer.

Rick ran into the house. There on the floor sat Marcus leaning back against the wall. He knelt by him. At first he thought he too was dead. But it was just his breathing. It was very shallow. He slapped him hard and yelled. It did no good. He grabbed up a bucket of water and threw at him. Marcus remained out. He was off somewhere. Far, far off.

Then he saw the note on the table. It was in Marta's handwriting but stiff, very stiff. It said: *Rick, it's all over. I must go. Marta.*

He ran outside. So many feelings racked through him now that he couldn't possibly categorize them, but his whole life's training came back to him in one thought straight and true.

He mounted and rode hard for town. About a mile from the edge of Two Mesas he reined off, taking a short cut on high ground through thick brush for Salt River. He reined up about two-thirds of a mile above Duvall's camp. He could see Duvall, Marta, and the Indian woman moving around below. He strained his eyes but couldn't spot the male Apache. He'd known Marta'd be here. There had been no question about that.

He clamped his jaws down and ground his teeth audibly as Red Spot picked his way down through the brush towards the camp. He wanted a surprise now, but he was worried about the Indian, One Lion. He had to win this. Losing Marta was only a part of it. His heir was going away in her lovely belly. A friend of his lay dead in the morgue, another was in Flag having a screw twisted into his shattered jaw bones, and old dog was dead. All this was enough but there was one other reason he rode forward and down. There was something that had to be removed from the earth. Something that had to be ripped and torn and turned back to dust.

It was the bunching of Red Spot's muscles that saved him. He caught the glimpse of One Lion moving in front of him through the brush before the Indian could level the gun to shoot. At the second he stepped between the two large bushes,

Rick jammed the spurs deep into the appaloosa's sides and laid forward on his neck. The horse lunged powerfully forward striking the Indian in the chest with eleven hundred pounds of hard-muscled force.

The gun fired in the air and it flew into the brush. Rick turned and rode the horse back and forth across the Indian and the meat peeled from his scalp and the bones crunched in his chest and shoved into his lungs. He was a part of Duvall and must be destroyed!

Then he rode on down the hill again, holding the excited horse in check. He caught a glimpse of Duvall coming up the hill in the blowing dust carrying a gun. *Damn, he was a fool. He should have known the Indian would be spotted there, waiting, guarding.* Rick hadn't even brought his gun, and now he'd lost the Indian's in the brush. Rage brings on foolish acts.

He could see Duvall's dark clothes coming closer now. He reined around behind a big cedar and waited. He took his rope down and tied it hard to his saddle horn and formed a calf-sized loop. Well, this is all he had. Hell, he wasn't much of a shot anyway. But he could fit this rope around a steer's neck in a small opening in thick brush at full horse speed. Why not this man's neck that he wanted now more than all the steers in the world.

The wind moaned and talked of life and death and love and for a moment it was touched with mocking laughter. He'd heard this wind all his life. It drove killing snow and ice. It shoved dust that mutilated the grass and vegetation. It also brought the spring rains and the summer storms and then always blew back to destruction. It was the same wind that had turned the windmills the day he was born, and he was sure it was the one sound that would penetrate his final grave.

He couldn't hear Duvall's steps for it now, but on the other hand it was a great equalizer—Duvall couldn't hear him.

He pulled back slightly on the reins and gripped Red Spot with his knees trying to tell him not to move—that all life depended on his not moving. The horse stood like a perfectly trained roping horse in a roping box. And then he saw the little blur of darkness on the other side of the tree, the horse's ears go forward, and felt him tremble, but he held.

Duvall stepped into the tiny clearing, crouched, the gun forward and cocked. It was too late! The rope shot out sure and clean around the neck. Rick jerked the slack tight and turned, reining and spurring hard downhill. He spurred the horse through trees and bushes in wild descent. He could feel the weight come and go as it hung and broke loose behind him. Suddenly the hill steepened and a thick growth of cedar rose right up before them. Their momentum was such that they splintered straight through them. Rick was almost knocked from the saddle but righted himself and held onto the rope. The wide shoulders of Duvall stuck in the forks of one of the cedars and for a fleeting second the horse and rider were checked. Then the rope pulled loose and free in his hand as they plunged downward to the camp. Something rolled past them and came to rest against the gleaming hub cap of the shining new car. And there its eyes stared up into the dust and sun-scorched sky. But they were filled with gravel and saw nothing, hypnotized nothing.

The two women stood staring at the head. Staring. Rick stepped down from Red Spot who breathed heavily from more than just the work.

Rick walked over to Marta. "Marta," he said.

She still looked at the head. She had no expression of horror, just nothing—like Duvall's face. Rick spoke her name again and again. Slowly she raised her head. Then her eyes widened. She leaped past Rick, grabbed a rock from the ground and hurled it into the face of the Apache woman. The woman fell and rolled over and sat up, her nose broken and bleeding. Rick saw the knife she'd dropped on the ground gleaming, clean, and unused. It had been meant for his back.

Marta knelt by the woman, took the edge of her dress and wiped the blood tenderly from her face.

"I'm sorry," she said. Then she stood up, looked at Rick, and said, "The Indian was *his* woman."

"Go on home. Drive Duvall's car," Rick said, "and take care of Marcus. I've got to go to town and tell the sheriff."

"Are you coming on home soon?" she asked.

"Yes, I'll be home soon," he said.

She walked towards the car. Well, it was over. She was Rick's forever. Nothing else could tear them apart now. No matter how he treated her, she was his. She started the car and drove down the road. Rick mounted, gathered up his rope, and rode towards town while the Indian woman stood staring, still, like old dog used to do, at the bottom of the wheel. The horse shied a bit as the yellow dress that had been ripped from the saddle blew across the ground. But Rick didn't see it.